Reina Explores the Zoo

Let's marvel at the beautiful creation!

By Sheila C. Duperrier
Illustrated by K.K.P. Dananjali

Reina Explores the Zoo

By Sheila C. Duperrier
ReinaZone.com:
The zone for innovative kids and fun learning!

Edition October 2022

Reina explores the Zoo
English (zo-EN)

While every precaution has been taken in the preparation of this book, the author and publisher assume no responsibility for errors or omissions, or for damages resulting from the use of the information contained herein.

Paperback ISBN: 978-1-958816-09-7
eBook ISBN: 978-1-958816-19-6

Copyright © 2022 Reinazone.com
All rights reserved.

Once there was a girl who loved to learn and explore.
Her name was *Reina*, and she wanted to know more and more.

So, one day, Mom and Dad invited her and her
little brother to the zoo.
When she heard that, Reina knew just what to do!
She invited Marc and Rose, her friends from school.
And they both thought that was really cool!

Off to the zoo, they went as the sun shone brightly.
They said hello to the workers very politely.
They learned to be safe and careful with all the animals at the zoo.
They listened to the workers and their parents, too.

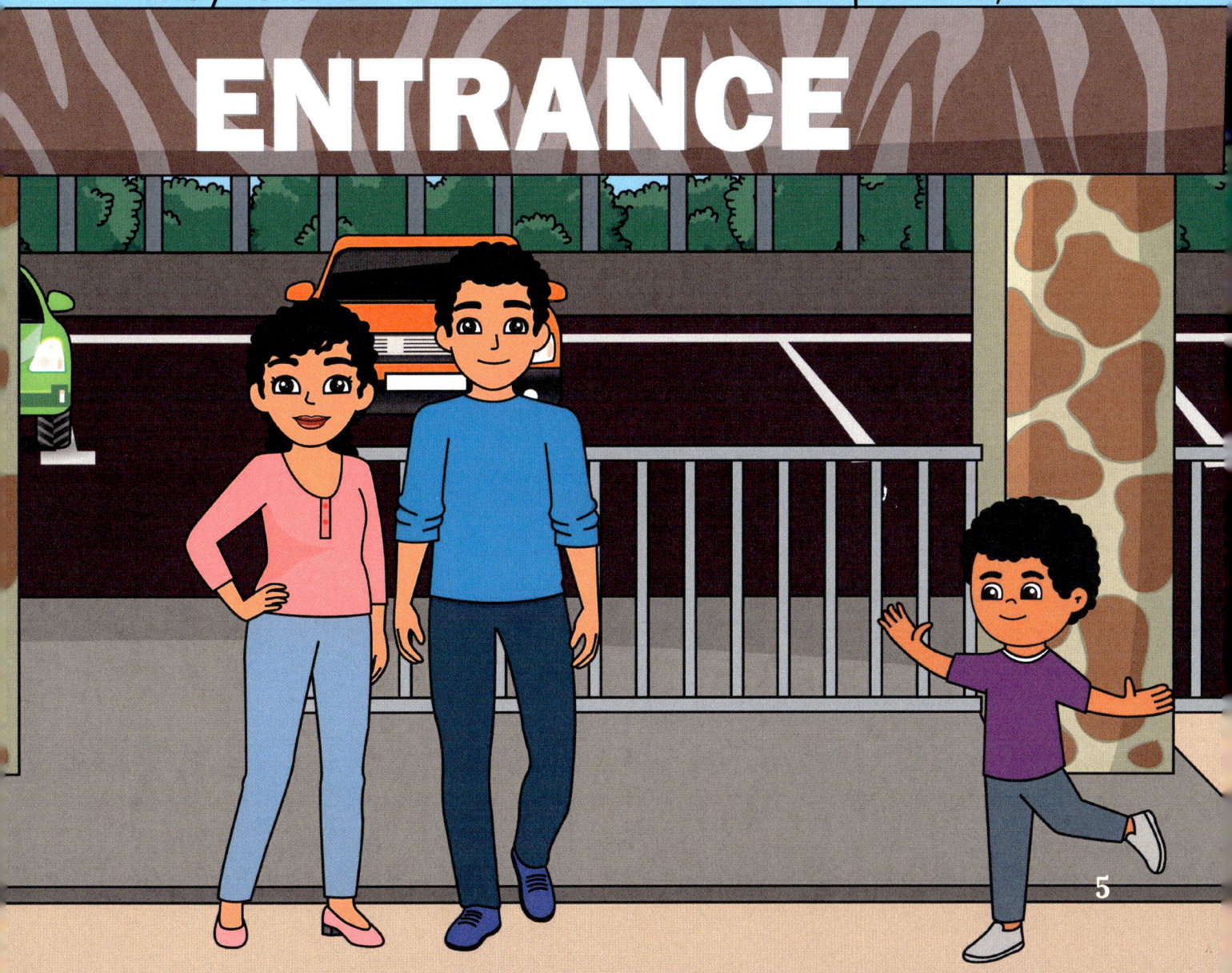

ENTRANCE

Dad pointed to where all the birds flew.
Then Reina clapped her hands and knew just what to do!
There were all kinds of new, feathery friends to meet.
They heard lots of chirps, whistles, and even a tweet!

Can you count all the birds you see?

Hyacinth macaws whistled and flew.
An **American black vulture** joined them, too!
An **Eastern Screech Owl** perched above.
There might even have been a **magpie** and **dove**!

There was a **Blue** and **Gold Macaw** so pretty and bright.
A **yellow-crowned Amazon** ruffled its feathers and took flight.
Then, a **Bald Eagle** spread its wings wide.
"This is all so amazing!" Reina cried.

Can you spot an animal that does not belong to this group?

Then it was off to the invertebrates, but what animal is that?
A cat? Maybe a bat?
Reina asked her dad, "what does invertebrate mean?"
"Those are bugs and worms and creepy crawlers," he said.
Reina and her friends were so excited that they ran ahead.

They saw **spiders**, **cockroaches**, and **millipedes**! They were crawling on branches, leaves, and even the weeds!

Spot an animal that has no leg.
Spot one that has a lot of legs.

Tarantulas with big hairy legs crawled by their side.
A hissing **cockroach** walked boldly with pride!

Could there be a **scorpion**, too?
"Stay away from them," said Dad. "That is what you do!"

If you were in Reina's place, what would you do?

Which ones of these fun creatures have you met already?

AMPHIBIANS

Reina knew where she wanted to go next.
She pointed to her map and read the text.
"The amphibians are slimy and cool!
Come see the **salamanders** and **frogs** in the pool!"

White Tree Frogs were peaceful and slow.
While the **Tiger Salamander** really stole the show!

What is your favorite reptile?

Then it was off to see the reptiles
—**snakes** and **lizards** that seemed to go on for miles and miles!

A **Jamaican Boa** slithered and hissed.
The American **crocodiles** and **alligators** couldn't be missed!

The **Giant Gecko** was a sight to see.
The Spotted Turtle was so cute and pretty.

We have all types of animals living in the wild.
So, it was time to go through their habitat in a ride.

Finally, there was one last exhibit to see.
"Should we see the mammals?"
asked Reina.
And everyone had to agree!

The mammals are related to
you and me.
They have warm blood, make
milk, and have hair
like a **monkey**, **tiger**, or **bear**!

The **black bear** was a big friendly guy.
He rolled over and reached up to the sky.

Do you see an animal with fur?

Can spot the animals from the text?

The **giraffes** had necks so very long and tall.
There were so big they made everyone else feel so very small!
The **leopards** had spots and lots of muscles to run.
The **goats**, **otters**, and **alpacas** were so much fun.

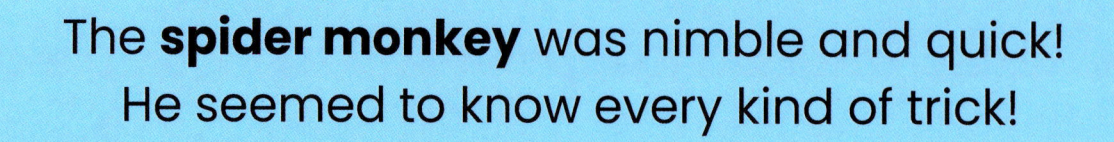

The **spider monkey** was nimble and quick!
He seemed to know every kind of trick!

The **two-toed sloth** was slow and sleepy.
The warthog was a bit scary and creepy.

The ride was so cool with lots to discover.
A lot of wonderful creatures to admire.
But there are more wonders to see.

The **cheetah** was fast, like lightning striking!
But the cute **lemur** was more to Reina's liking.

Which creature is the fastest runner on earth?

The **elephants** were slow and strong.
Their trunks were big and really long!

Can you spot the biggest land animal?

Finally, it was time to go.
So Reina, her little brother, and friends
said goodbye to every **bird**, **snake**, **elephant**, and **hen**.
Everyone couldn't wait to come back again!

Reina marveled at the beautiful, colorful creation and promised to protect the environment and animals in every nation!

Author's note:

Thank you very much for exploring the Zoo with Reina. If you enjoyed it, please consider leaving a review on the site you get it and/or on ReinaZone.com. Don't forget to recommend it to a friend.

To get the accompanying coloring book
Search for "Reina Explores the Zoo – Coloring Book"
This awesome coloring book is packed with more than 50 fun creatures! It will be a perfect gift for a child. **Get your copy today**.

Visit ReinaZone.com for more information.
Scan the QR code below to **get your gift now**.
Thank you again for your support.

- Sheila C. Duperrier

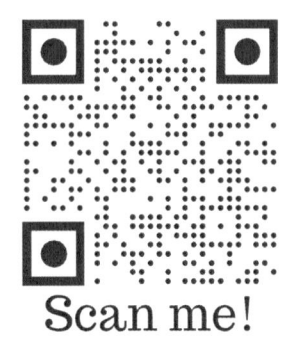

Scan me!